DEATHLY DELIGHTS

Deathly Delights

STORIES BY

Anne Dandurand

TRANSLATED BY
LUISE VON FLOTOW

Véhicule Press

MONTRÉAL

Translated and published with the assistance of The Canada Council.
Fiction series editor: Linda Leith
Cover design and artwork: JW Stewart
Design and imaging: ECW Type & Art
Printing: Les Editions Marquis Ltée

CANADIAN CATALOGUING IN PUBLICATION DATA

Dandurand, Anne, 1953–
  Deathly delights

Translation of: L'assassin de l'intérieur et Diables d'espoir which
  were published together, back to back, without a collective title.
ISBN 1-55065-022-X

I. Title.

PS8557.A52A8713 1991   C843'.54   C91-090602-5
PQ3919.2.D36A8713 1991

Véhicule Press, P.O.B. 125, Place du Parc Station, Montreal,
Quebec H2W 2M9

Canadian distribution
University of Toronto Press, 5201 Dufferin Street,
Downsview, Ontario M3H 5T8

U.S. distribution
University of Toronto Press (Buffalo, NY); Inland Book Company
(East Haven, CT); and Bookslinger Inc. (St. Paul, MN).

Printed in Canada on acid-free paper.

CONTENTS

PART I

Tu es l'arme
qui t'achèvera

— Yves Gosselin
Brescia, miracle de la justice amère

Inside Killer

SUNDAY, NOVEMBER 15

It's snowing already. Real suicide weather. Eight years of hell, day in day out. Monday to Friday, every day, my boss strokes my ass.

I've talked to him. I've raged at him. I've cried. Nothing works. I'm a prisoner. My boss, Robert Lalancette, denies everything and increases my pay. My salary no longer reflects my skills, and with rampant unemployment, I can't give up the job; I'd never find anything as good.

Today I'm starting my journal again, after eight years. To write my life before I explode.

So, I am the prisoner of my boss, his money and my shame.

NOVEMBER 16

He won't even admit he touches me. He protests his innocence in the tones of an offended virgin. I am tired of fighting emptiness.

I don't understand it. I'm no beauty and over the

9

years I have even forced myself to become dowdy. I only wear baggy clothes, brown or black.

But nothing changes.

This evening when I got home, it was strange—the radio wasn't playing.

NOVEMBER 17

Tonight the radio was off again when I got in. But it does work. I know I set it at a rock station before I left this morning. Most days I'm greeted with classical music when I get home, but this time I thought that rock might help dispel my uneasiness.

At 5:30 though, there was nothing. I checked the locks on the doors and windows right away. Nothing unusual.

I'm a little worried.

NOVEMBER 18, 7:00 A.M.

In spite of my fears I slept heavily and didn't dream. A fresh shock this morning, though. During the night, someone turned off the fluorescent lights in my book-case. That's where I keep my doll collection. If I wake up, their fixed smiles reassure me.

I feel panicky now. It's been snowing and snowing. No footprints. In a frenzy, I searched the remotest corners of the house before I left. I called the police; they laughed at me.

Actually, it's absurd—a radio that goes off by itself and a light over a doll collection that does the same thing.

This evening I came home feeling very apprehensive. What a relief to hear Vivaldi on Radio-Canada. But that was only a momentary reprieve. On the floor next to my bed, I found a pair of black silk stockings attached to a garter belt. They were laid out like the open legs of a woman.

A cousin gave the stockings and garter belt to me as a joke years ago. I have never worn them — they're not my style. I didn't even know I had them anymore.

They looked like an obscene grimace and gave off a stench of cigarette butts and sweat. They've been worn: the heels are dirty, the knees baggy. I tried to think but my head was spinning. I took refuge in a hotel, with a fierce migraine.

THE 19TH, IN THE MORNING

It's no better at the hotel. The clothes I carefully folded yesterday evening are soiled with a sticky kind of grease. The sleeves are knotted and the underwear ripped.

I don't know what to think. I stayed motionless for a long time, my heart bursting out of my chest, a taste of rust in my mouth.

I finally called the hotel management who assured me of the hotel's security. When you lock your room from the inside, no one can get in.

And this morning the bolt was in place.

NOVEMBER 20

I returned home. I am frightened. Who is following me? I live alone, without any friends. I spend all my money on my precious doll collection. Why me?

Everything seems quiet, but I no longer trust anything.

NOVEMBER 23, IN THE MORNING

I sat indoors all weekend. For what? I don't know. Every evening I slipped into the heavy sleep which is beginning to puzzle me. But when I try to think about this abnormal torpor I get confused and can't concentrate. I vaguely see a door in the mist, but like in a dream, every effort to reach it draws me further away . . . At least nothing has happened.

THE 23RD, AROUND NOON

This morning at the office, the police were waiting for me. My boss, Robert Lalancette, was strangled last night with a black silk stocking. I thought I'd faint. I answered the inspector's questions. Yes, his business was flourishing; no, I didn't know of any enemies; then I rushed home. Obviously I have only one black stocking left.

NOVEMBER 24

I have a week off. Madame Lalancette said she would take care of the business after she made the funeral arrangements. I had the impression she didn't particularly like the deceased either. She was so calm, even hiding a smile. She was visiting her sister in Boston the night of the murder. She told me she didn't really understand the motive for the killing. It couldn't have been theft; nothing was taken.

Madame Lalancette was talking to me, but all of a sudden I had difficulty hearing her. I was fascinated by her unusual face and her long neck. She batted her eyelids very slowly like one of those cruel carnivorous plants, a Venus flytrap.

When she left, I stayed I don't know how long, breathing in her perfume which hung like a scarf in the dusty office. And all the noise of the jungle deafened me.

NOVEMBER 25

Nothing strange the last two nights. Here I am figuring normal and abnormal days.

I cleaned everything today, washed everything, got rid of everything useless that's been weighing me down. I would have sprinkled the walls with holy water only I haven't believed in anything for a long time.

I'm finished. The whole place smells of wax, vinegar and ammonia.

I found a small photo of Jean-Pierre stuck between the floorboards.

I look at it. It tears me apart inside. And yet, I've spent eight years hardening myself. I wasn't even thinking about him any more. I was even forgetting to tell myself I had forgotten about him.

I have a a taste of sand in my mouth. Why did he

leave my life so abruptly. Why did he just vanish as though he only ever existed in my head?

He went out for milk and disappeared. I looked for him. I cried. I never even found out if he died. I decided to close myself off. I took the monotonous job with Lalancette. I concentrated on becoming a shadow of myself, a skinny little old maid with no desires and a manic passion for porcelain dolls.

Lalancette with his roaming hands and his stupid tactics was an easy person to hate, so petty next to my suffering.

I look at the photo and then I see a sign. What if it's Jean-Pierre? He used to like frightening me.

I never changed the locks and he left with the key, eight years ago.

NOVEMBER 26

I woke up very late even though I went to sleep early.

"He" came again last night. My dolls were moved. The three Bye-Lo dolls were strung up by their feet. My little Brue, so cute in her flowered hat, was floating in the toilet. The Frozen Charlottes were lined up like slices of bacon in a frying pan. The eighteen Pierrots were drowning in the garbage can among greasy bits of paper and carrot scrapings. Desecrated.

I spent the day washing, starching and ironing tiny clothes. Everything is back to normal, but the fear won't leave me.

If it is Jean-Pierre what is he trying to tell me? And if it isn't Jean-Pierre, who is it?

NOVEMBER 27

A normal night, except for this heavy dreamless sleep. Around five o'clock I went to see my neighbour in the back. I don't like her very much. She teaches nursery school. I run into her occasionally in the morning or in the evening. She's always exhausted, as though her brats engaged her in merciless combat, or as though some secret vice devoured her nights.

I grew tired of having coffee with her — I had the feeling that I was listening to a broken record. She hates her sisters, her colleagues, her friends. After a couple of hours she even had bad things to say about Jean-Pierre, whom she'd known at university.

But today I went to find out if she'd noticed anything strange at my place.

After listening to the usual complaints, I discovered that she had actually seen a man go in my back door, around four on the morning of the 26th.

He'd had a key, and she hadn't seen him leave. Now at least I know I'm not crazy.

NOVEMBER 28

I walked the streets today. It reminded me of the time Jean-Pierre disappeared. The clear sky hurt my eyes; I walked on the shady side of the street all day.

I systematically criss-crossed the centre of town like I did eight years ago. After Jean-Pierre left I went to the morgue day after day, for six months, checking the unidentified corpses. I spent the rest of the time looking for him. I would stare at every man I met. I told myself that if Jean-Pierre had lost his memory, he must surely be wandering around somewhere in the bowels of the city. It was time wasted.

At the corner of St. Laurent and Ste. Catherine, an outrageous young transvestite stepped into my path. He said, "Heh Réal, how come you're dressed up like a woman today?" Then he planted a kiss on my mouth and took off, laughing.

Is he connected with this mystery?

Réal who?

NOVEMBER 29

I went to buy a doll. My favourite dealer, a dwarf, muttered behind my back, "*Tu hueles a la muerte, mi bella!*" It sent chills down my spine.

On the way home I pressed the doll to me like a talisman. On the bus I found a *Journal de Montréal* wedged between my seat and the wall. I haven't read the papers for a long time. Why did I glance at that one? What obscure desire pushed me to my ruin?

I immediately recognized his picture on page two. Someone strangled my transvestite last night.

NOVEMBER 30, IN THE EVENING

This morning around 5:00 "he" tried to burn down the neighbour's house.

She wasn't sleeping. She saw the same man she'd seen on the night of the 26th. He was wearing the same cape and black hat. She wasn't able to see his face in the dark. He tossed some old papers on the doorstep, sprinkled them with what appeared to be lighter fluid, and then deliberately lit a cigarette which he threw on to the pile. Then he quickly went into my house, using his key.

After he had gone my neighbour was able to put out the fire, but her oak door will always be charred.

The police arrived to question me. I couldn't tell them anything. I'd slept like a corpse. In spite of the fresh snow, there were no footprints on my pink carpet or on the pine floors. The police searched the house and found nothing.

They've gone now, leaving me with my terror.

I don't understand.

Jean-Pierre and I were in love with each other when he left. So why would he be angry with me?

On the other hand, if he's gone crazy, or if it's someone else, it's up to me alone to find some way to escape this.

DECEMBER FIRST

It's raining. It smells of poverty and exhaustion outside.

I went to the hardware store to buy some electric wire, a large iron wash tub, a set of large insulated "alligator" clips, a four-foot-square piece of carpet, and a long copper pipe that I had bent for me into a circle five feet in diameter.

I worked the rest of the day setting my trap.

For the first time in two weeks I fell asleep with peace in my heart.

Murder or Mysterious Suicide?

Alerted by a neighbour who noticed a strange odour, officers of the Quebec Police have made a macabre discovery.

In the cellar of 9797 rue de la Visitation they have found the remains of Blanche Bellemare, a resident at that address, in a state of advanced decomposition.

The circumstances of her death remain unclear. Lieutenant Marc Mongeau has reconstructed what may have happened. When the victim entered her home, she tumbled into the cellar through an open trap door hidden by a small rug. Just below the trap door was a large tub of brine into which she fell. In an attempt to catch her balance, she must have caught hold of a copper hoop suspended horizontally midway between the floor and the basement ceiling. Since the copper hoop was soldered to an electric wire plugged into the fuse box, Blanche Bellemare was electrocuted by a charge of 220 volts.

The mystery grows more complicated as we try to find a motive for the murder, or reasons for the suicide. A charred notebook was discovered on the premises.

The police are also puzzled by the men's clothing the dead woman was wearing, specifically a cape and a black hat, as well as by the collection of dolls lined up like spectators on the smooth dirt floor of the cellar.

Exit the Ex

June 15, 11:11 p.m.

Christophe settles into his favourite armchair. Actually it's the only one he owns. Nina used to cover it with a quilt — one of the things that she took away with her when they split up. Under his thighs, the fabric on the seat is as threadbare as an old wound.

It is oppressively hot. Montreal is weighed down by a humidity unusual for the end of spring. The slightly-deranged landlady upstairs is vacuuming. Christophe's landing is quiet. The homosexual must have gone out. (Nina affectionately nicknamed him the ghost, because you hear him more often than you see him.) The manic-depressive filmmaker downstairs moved out a week go. Predictably, from the window of the other downstairs apartment, Nina's radio is pouring out its deafening torrent of heavy rock.

That's been her mania since the break-up, listening to non-stop rock, even at night. And she wears her Walkman when she goes out.

From behind the painted shirt that serves as a curtain,

Christophe sometimes watches her. It is so easy to keep track of her comings and goings; she always turns down the volume on her radio before she goes out. For three days now Nina has been spitting on Christophe's doorstep.

He listens carefully. Suddenly David Bowie is singing more quietly. The door slams, ten hurried clicks of the heels resonate in the silent street, and then comes the sound of a throat being cleared.

More spit on his doorstep. Where is Nina going at this late hour? All at once he is worried; he knows how suicide attracts her. It's stifling in here; why not follow her, just in case?

June 16, 1:17 a.m.

She took narrow, dingy alleys through the east end, slipped through a condemned underpass, and then turned off towards the railway yards near the river. She's sitting on a broken cement block now, smoking her second cigarette.

Christophe is watching her from behind a derelict railway car. He's waiting. For what? He doesn't know himself. Is she crying? In the distance a bus howls mournfully.

A policeman, or a security guard, appears from between two warehouses and limps towards Nina. She points her finger in Christophe's direction. Does she know he followed her?

The guard approaches Christophe. Paralyzed, a little shameful, he hopes he won't be found. The policeman calls him. Of course, he will stop bothering her and go home.

Nina has dissolved into the night.

June 17, 4:49 a.m., the grey hour

Christophe is tangled in his sheets. He is dreaming of a twisted, dark house full of trap doors. He wants to escape. His hands are covered in blood.

The telephone rings. Christophe wakes up with relief. He answers. No sound on the other end. It's the fifth time tonight. It's probably Nina. The Stones are pounding into the receiver and also from her apartment. Furious, Christophe yells, "Stop it, Nina, cut it out. I'll kill you, if you don't stop it, Nina!"

The phone goes dead. Sweating, Christophe is upset that he let himself get carried away. Outside, Nina's prolonged laughter rips through the moist night.

June 25, 2:13 p.m.

Christophe is back from a short trip out of town. He feels better. At least he hasn't had to avoid Nina all week. It is complicated living next door to a woman you once loved.

As he enters his apartment he's struck by a vile smell. He looks around. Eustache, Nina's ginger cat, lies rotting on the bed.

How did she get in? Nina gave him back her keys, but she knows how to unlatch the back window. Would she imprison her beloved cat in Christophe's place to have it die of thirst? But why? And besides, the window was repaired while he was away.

Christophe vomits. Trembling, he leans on the table. A new mystery. A week ago he pulled the Hermit, the Juggler, the Lover and the Wheel of Fortune from the Tarot pack. Now it's the Tower, the Moon, the Hanged Man and Death.

Nina?

June 26, 5:23 a.m.

She has phoned again. Seven times during the night. If it really is Nina. Christophe is exhausted: the heat, these silent calls, he can't find his strength.

It's been seven weeks since the break-up and Nina can't seem to calm down. Christophe sighs. With meagre welfare payments and his few, small contracts, it's hard to survive, let alone move. He'll have to manage. What will she come up with next?

June 27, noon.

Christophe gazes at the telephone. Nina has begged him to meet her tonight at midnight at her place. One last time. She was crying so hard that he ended up agreeing. The front door will be unlocked, she said.

She gave an odd little laugh before she hung up. Christophe felt chilled for an hour.

the 27th, midnight

At Nina's place, above the rock music that is blaring more loudly than ever, Christophe hears dull blows and moans. He opens the door. On the floor there is a kitchen knife just like one of his own. He has no time to think about this. Nina is shrieking, "Christophe, help! Help!"

He seizes the knife and rushes into the living room at the back of the apartment. The furniture is overturned, the dolls are in pieces. In Nina's place such disorder is a real shock.

Seated in her armchair, Nina pivots to face him. She is alone, naked, and mortally wounded. Musical staves are painted all over her body. Nina is a great fugue, stabbed from her throat to her sex. She whispers, "Good bye, my love; you can't escape me any more." And her laugh ends in a frightful gurgle.

June 28, 3:21 a.m.

Christophe has been wandering around the bus terminal for hours in a daze. He just dropped the knife at Nina's feet and ran. He's waiting for the first bus for St-Jean-Port-Joli, where he'll take refuge with his only friend. He needs time to think.

July 2, 11:09 a.m.

At the café La Coureuse des grèves, in St-Jean-Port-Joli Christophe is startled by the front page of *Montréal Matin*. There it is. They've found Nina and are looking for him. He pays for his espresso, and makes his way back to Montreal.

July 3, 1:47 a.m.

Christophe leaves the police station on rue Parthenais. To his great surprise they let him go. His fingerprints are on the knife. He has no alibi. Why didn't he notify the police? Why did he quit town? The detective, a man about his age named Marc Mongeau, treated him politely, despite his suspicions. Christophe is not to leave the city again.

July 3, 10:00 a.m. on the dot
The doorbell rings. It is Lieutenant Mongeau, fresh as a daisy. With his shoulders bent, Christophe offers him a coffee. Mongeau refuses. He inspects the apartment, goes through the papers on the table; the questions begin again.

"Have you already been unfaithful to Nina?"

"No."

"Why did she keep her apartment downstairs?"

"She wanted her own space, even if it was just for her doll collection."

"Did she earn a comfortable living ?"

"Yes, very. Much better than I do."

"Did you owe her any money?"

"Yes, about a thousand dollars. I wanted to pay her back as soon as possible."

Mongeau smiles sceptically, and pulls some musical scores off the bookshelf. You never know.

In the top of the kitchen cupboard, in a messy pile of dishcloths and sheets, the detective finds an envelope. Christophe moves closer, intrigued. In it are about thirty polaroid shots of Nina, naked and in pornographic poses.

"Who took these photos?"

"Not me."

"What are they doing here?"

"I don't know anything about them. I didn't even know I had them."

The doorbell rings. The mailman with a welfare cheque and a registered letter. Christophe signs for it, with the Lieutenant waiting patiently at his shoulder.

A letter from Nina.

> *Christophe, I don't want to give you any more money. I don't give a damn about the photos; publish them if you want. If you talk to me one more time, I'll call the police. Why did you kill my cat?*
>
> *Nina.*

The motive had been missing. Mongeau smiles; the air thickens; Christophe cringes.

"Would you please come with me? You're under arrest."

July 4, late afternoon

From behind bars Christophe is watching life pass by. His cell allows him five steps in one direction, three in the other. He could sit on the bed or on the toilet bowl. He doesn't want to. Mongeau stares at him.

"Why are you on welfare if you've got seventeen thousand dollars?"

"I don't understand."

"You don't have seventeen thousand dollars in your bank account?"

"No. For months now I've been cashing my cheque without looking at the balance. Too depressing."

"So who made deposits of eight thousand five hundred dollars on the 18th and the 23rd of June?"

Christophe grows pale.

"Nina, maybe?"

The kind of silence that precedes an earthquake falls between them. Christophe clenches his teeth to prevent himself from sobbing. Marc Mongeau touches his shoulder.

"You know, they always assign me to the weird cases. What's strange about yours is the way the clues are so obvious. You're too clumsy to be a killer."

Mongeau calls the guard and leaves. Christophe grips the bars of his cell as tightly as if he were trying to squeeze hope out of them.

July 5, dawn

The city begins to stir. Listening to footsteps, sighs, and the ever-present sounds of clanking metal, Christophe hasn't slept. He is innocent; there has to be a flaw somewhere in this trap.

But Nina's laugh racks him like a toothache.

July 6, just before noon

With his schoolboy grin and his snake eyes, Lieutenant Mongeau asks him:

"The good news or the bad news?"

"The bad news."

"Jeanne Couteau and some of her friends have testified that Nina complained indirectly about you and your blackmailing. They all talked about how Nina was afraid of you. When I look at you, I can't believe them

. . . but they're not lying . . . so it's Nina who . . ."

The Lieutentant pauses. A snippet of hope and already Christophe can hear the sea, smell the salt air. Mongeau is watching him.

"Now the good news. The window through which Nina is supposed to have gained entry into your place, sometime between the 18th and the 25th of June—that window was fixed. Nina could not have got in that way. It was repaired recently, and not by the landlady — I asked her. You don't know how to do anything with your hands, I suppose, except play the piano?"

"That's right."

"But we found tools and materials at your place, hidden away. You didn't want Nina to get in any more because of the photos, right?"

Christophe has no answers left; an enormous vise is closing in on him. Nina thought of everything. She always did think of everything.

Mongeau leaves. He's had all he can take for one day. He can't watch this kid flounder any longer.

Christophe stretches out on the thin mattress, his palms over his eyes. Suddenly the concrete smells of Nina's perfume, and if he holds still he can feel her hair tickling his neck. Christophe tries to close himself off, and Nina finally whispers her distress in his ear.

July 7, morning

"Get up! There is something odd about your scores. Do you remember the music written across Nina's body?"

Christophe opens his eyes with the feeling of entering a familiar nightmare. But Lieutenant Marc Mongeau, with his starched shirt and his Brut after-shave, doesn't let him escape reality for long.

"I was too shocked to look closely at Nina's body."

"It's an exact copy of the third movement of one of your pieces, "Ultima Thule." An unpublished piece?"

"Yes."

Mongeau sighs.

"So that excludes suicide, unless one of her friends painted the score on her back for her. But everyone denies it. You'll have a lot of difficulty with that one in front of the judge."

Christophe smiles at him. The night has brought him understanding. Nina has explained it all to him. There's no more need to struggle to prove his innocence. No one will believe him. He doesn't believe it himself anymore.

December, one evening

From his cell, Christophe contemplates the stars. He didn't love Nina enough. He's been given the maximum sentence and it's not too high a price to pay. She's always at his side now. All day-long they talk in low voices and lie in each other's arms all night. Nina is happy now and laughs often.

The other prisoners call him "crackpot," but Christophe couldn't care less. He's in love with Nina again.

Lost Hearts Salon

Marc Mongeau shivered and turned up the collar of his coat. It was getting near Christmas and still raining. In the mornings the metro smelled of damp newspapers and unwashed bodies. Lieutenant Marc Mongeau could have afforded a car, but he preferred the metro which allowed him to speculate about the secret cares of his fellow passengers. Since he could never check his findings, he had the impression that he was never wrong.

The metro made up for his work in the police force where for years now he'd been assigned the most intricate cases. Even when he managed to solve a case, worrying doubts about the real motives and nature of the supposed killers continued to gnaw at him. These doubts left his eyes creased with insomnia.

He went straight down to the morgue on the third basement level. The red floor was still shiny from its last scrubbing with disinfectant. The only person who did not ignore him was the old morgue assistant who worked on autopsies. As usual she was reading technical charts for airplane engines in her windowless cubicle, her feet up on the desk. She raised her heavy eyelids to him.

"Nothing for you this morning, Marc. Two bikers who knifed each other to death; a vagrant they found on Saint-Jacques; and an old lady who died at the Hôtel Dieu. And then . . ."

Her words faded away into a sad daydream. No one knew anything about the morgue assistant except that she could always be called in an emergency because she never went out. But then she continued murmuring, almost to herself it seemed. "And then there's that guy, a good-looking fellow too, about thirty, who broke his neck when he fell onto a cement sculpture in his apartment. It was his girlfriend who called us, in tears."

"So? Why do you mention him?"

"He fell because he received an electric shock. He's the third in two months. The other two were about the same age, and all three were alone at home in their locked apartments when they were electrocuted. Odd, isn't it?"

"Yes, but I can hardly see myself explaining to the boss that I want an inquiry into three accidents."

The morgue assistant turned back to her engine charts. "Oh? I thought it might interest you. Never mind then . . ."

Marc Mongeau took a detour through the refrigerators anyway. The shock victim, with his neck twisted at an atrocious angle, still had his eyes wide open in surprise.

10:50 a.m. There's a steady drizzle. Calabrini, who

shares an office with Mongeau, is on the first floor questioning a woman who killed her lover in front of witnesses two days ago in a club. The others always have an easier time of it.

No air, the windows are sealed tight and there's already half a pack of Mark Ten reeking in the ashtray. Mongeau struggles with drowsiness, resentful that it should elude him at night. He shakes himself and goes to wash his hands for the sixth time since his arrival.

In the washroom the white of the tiled walls screams under the neon lights. The water is cold, and so real. Mongeau rinses his eyes. For a brief moment the corpse he saw in the morning opens its mouth in the mirror. He's so tired he's hallucinating, that's all. But it's not coming back to him for nothing. The dead man seemed to be asking such an urgent question that Mongeau gives in. He'll see about an inquiry.

With a great clicking of his dentures, the boss refuses. It's his opinion the three cases are just accidents, even though there are similarities. Mongeau acquiesces, but outside office hours his time is his own.

12:15 p.m. Rather than have the cafeteria version of ravioli for lunch, Mongeau is on the eleventh floor chewing on a piece of kleenex. The computer is spitting out the circumstances surrounding the electrocution of the three men. There seems to be no common thread.

The first victim, Jean Martineau, thirty-seven, was a heroin addict who had been let out on a temporary pass. On October 15th, in his bathtub, too high to think straight, he tried to replace an overhead lightbulb. His girlfriend, Elisabeth Thériault, was visiting her mother at the time.

The second, Pierre Joyal, thirty-three years old, was a taxidermist, and obese to boot. On November 8th, while shaving after his shower, he was electrocuted by a short circuit in his old razor when he plugged it into an unapproved wall socket. His wife, Charlotte Carrière was attending an evening course at the fatal moment.

And this morning's case, Marc Chartrand, thirty-five, was a musician. He had the bad luck to grab hold of a mike that was hooked up the wrong way. His guitar was too. Old instruments with no grounds. The shock threw Marc Chartrand on to a cement sculpture situated behind him. His latest conquest, France Varrin, lives in Matane, and arrived just as the macabre discovery was made.

Marc Mongeau suddenly discovers that his kleenex tastes disgusting.

Three days later, on a Sunday morning, the cold holds the city in its grip; frost glazes the sidewalks. In the implacable light silhouettes turn into thickly wrapped shadows. Mongeau has just returned from Matane. He didn't sleep at all during the long trip. In the bus terminal restaurant he bites into a piece of pie smothered with a layer of cream that is as questionable as his coffee.

The three women he has questioned have nothing in common either. One designs sets for television, another is a prospective real estate agent, the third a playwright. And they all have alibis of reinforced concrete. Except that each one feels some relief at the death of her man.

Elisabeth couldn't leave her Jean Martineau, in spite of the thefts and all the problems he caused her. She wanted to save him.

Pierre Joyal lied and was unfaithful to Charlotte, who continued to believe she could change him.

And though France Varrin fell in love with Marc Chartrand at first sight, she had some misgivings when she heard that his previous lover had committed suicide.

Three women more or less unhappy in love. Three more. Mongeau stretches, and his aches and pains subside as though appeased.

On the evening of the same day, Mongeau has thawed and devoured a meal of mock turkey. The usual calamities are pouring out of the television and his two-and-a-half rooms, in eggshell beige, are closing in on him. In the smoke wreaths from his sixty-third cigarette, Marc Mongeau suddenly sees the flowing hair of the three women.

Charlotte's—sleek as a blade, chestnut discreetly brushed with aubergine.

Elisabeth's—a surge of blonde silk with ash, almost pearly highlights.

France's—black and soft as an ominous cloud.

With three phone calls, Mongeau unearths the only real clue, the only link: all three women have their hair done at the Lost Hearts Salon. The heart as object. Marc Mongeau's liquid laughter drowns out the news reports on the famine.

Tuesday, 5:13 p.m. Lieutenant Mongeau has not been able to get an earlier appointment for a haircut. From the outside there is nothing special about the place. A neighbourhood hair salon like any other. Inside everything is turquoise.

He pushes open the door and goes inside. Why does he shiver at the sound of the Chinese chimes, as though he were at the edge of an abyss? The hairdresser approaches him. Her spiked hair makes her look like an insect and she's dressed in the same hues as her salon. A client with headphones on is drying her hair, her eyes closed, under infra-red lamps.

"What can I do for you, Lieutenant?"

"Odd name for a hair salon."

"Yes, it brings in a bizarre clientele . . . So, what would you like?"

Two hours later, after a scented shampoo, a meticulous haircut, a careful manicure, and after he has confided all the rancour of his life, Marc Mongeau is in love with Adrienne. He knows practically nothing about her and yet he has willingly revealed all the secrets of his heart to her.

The week has dissolved into drizzle and with it his colleagues, the station, and the details of the case. Marc dreams of Adrienne. Her voice, the trembling in Adrienne's voice. Marc gets lost in imagining what she might cry out during orgasm.

And in his dreams he opens the door again and again, and savours the little song of the Chinese chimes. It's a peculiar salon, with all those wigged heads above the mirrors, each with a different face. Adrienne must have painted them.

Reality cools Marc Mongeau down when he gets to this point. Beside the cash register is the grinding machine used for copying keys.

As she massaged his fingers, Adrienne did give him a plausible explanation for this. There are a lot of single-parent families in the area and many latch-key kids, as well as many old people. And therefore a lot of lost keys. It's a service, she said. The machine screeches; the dead grimace behind it.

Eleven days later, Thursday, 5:11 p.m. Lieutenant Marc Mongeau has just completed his most dangerous mission: over the phone he has made a date with Adrienne. It's for Saturday, and only at 11:00 p.m. Adrienne has to do somebody's hair at home. Taking his sleepless nights into consideration, that makes more than fifty-four hours to wait.

She said, "I'll see you at the Scratch," a bar he doesn't know on St. Denis. A cellar, with a ceiling at forehead level, walls painted in garish colours, tubes of black light. Why here? But she's coming down the staircase. There she is. In her presence the Scratch becomes as touching as a wound. She doesn't drink; she smokes lights; she listens to him. Marc finds amusing anecdotes, talks too much, and gets tangled up. He is thinking about the first kiss he'll give her.

They say goodbye two hours later. Marc is not disappointed. He'll see her again on Monday evening. She has less work on Mondays. He can wait. Beneath her silences he has sensed a pain that took a long time to heal and he doesn't want to rush her. She's invited him to her place on Monday.

He sleeps all day Sunday lying with his bedroom curtains wide open. He sleeps and dreams deliciously of being devoured by a big cat with turquoise eyes.

Monday evening. Mongeau's a little apprehensive. Adrienne opens the door to her apartment and smiles at him. He goes inside. Spider webs drape the corners of the apartment. He is amazed. She asks him to be careful near the desk: a new resident, tiny and red, has spun her web under the desk lamp. Adrienne moves closer and with the end of a pencil taps the outer edge of the web lightly with a rhythm that resembles a code. The spider wakes up and runs up the pencil right into Adrienne's hand.

"See? I tame them."

"Why?"

"I find them touching, with that thread coming out of their bellies that they weave into homes, and traps."

"But they devour their males."

Adrienne is still smiling, suddenly a little weary.

"Only the ones that don't bring them gifts."

In a flash Marc Mongeau understands. Now he knows. It was Adrienne who committed the murders. All the pieces fall into place. She was able to copy the women's keys while they sat with their headphones and couldn't hear what she was doing. Then she visited the three men's apartments and must have observed all their routines. A faulty appliance here, a loose lightbulb there, and then a dangerous connection—three perfect crimes that he will never be able to prove.

Marc Mongeau sighs, but he's happy. He knows that Adrienne wanted to help her clients, to extricate them from an intimate hell. Marc Mongeau finally takes Adrienne into his arms, whispering his love to her, kissing her, promising never to betray her. She laughs and lets herself go, but not without threatening to kill him if he ever breaks his promise.

Wednesday, early afternoon. It is snowing gently, muffling the noise of the city. Marc Mongeau, with a turquoise lock of hair dangling across his forehead, has tendered his resignation to the Police without explanation. All he said was that he was going into hairstyling.

Needless Fires

There isn't always work for him in the hair salon in the evenings. The opposite is true of the woman he loves, so he kills time in bars; he never goes back to the same one twice; and he never drinks anything except tall glasses of Perrier. He just listens to what others have to say and observes them secretly. He doesn't understand questions of the heart, his own included. Why is he not happy? Evening after evening he waits for an answer from a stranger's mouth.

It's raining. He always goes on foot because he is in no hurry. He breathes in the sweetish smell of rotting leaves. Why can't he get himself out of this state of limbo?

This evening he's decided to go to La Dépendance, a bar in the west end, the English part of town. The place is overflowing with noisy students, and only at the back, sheltered from the blaring loudspeakers, does he find a free seat beside a woman who would be pretty if her face weren't ruined by dark blue rings under her eyes.

She's wearing a scarlet silk blouse that reveals the top of her small breasts. She looks at her watch too insistently, lights a cigarette as if her life depended on it, and inhales deeply.

He says, "May I sit down?"

Very wearily, too wearily, she agrees.

The waiter, a young black man, as beautiful as a myth, brings her a cognac that she knocks back in one gulp, and him a glass of mineral water without ice.

He senses that she's going to talk to him. He waits patiently. Her voice is astonishingly solemn when she asks, "What is love?"

He doesn't reply. He thinks about the woman he loves, her unbroken cry when he enters her, her gaze filtered and shining, revealing its depths. Other images of her follow at once — her sinuous salamander belly, her crackling sex, her way of biting his hand between his thumb and forefinger, her clear morning smile. He thinks about the woman he loves and has doubts about himself. What does he know about love? He doesn't say anything, and the woman purses her lips triumphantly at his silence. In the end he admits, "Nobody knows anymore. I thought I knew. Tonight, I'm not sure of anything."

She's looked at her watch again, pricked up her ears, and shivered. Her secret seems so heavy, so cold, amid humanity so pathetic without direction, without hope, godless. Do the ones who escape despair have their eyes shut forever? He came here to find answers to his life, and instead more questions are crowding in on him. He gets up to leave, to breathe, and to find the only palpable truth, the long winter closing in. But she puts her hand on his arm and holds him back, ''Stay, I have to talk.''

She signals the waiter who wordlessly brings another round of drinks. She looks at her watch again and then begins in quite a completely different voice, distant and blank.

''I love the smell of flames and gunpowder. It's a pure hot scent, intoxicating, a fragrance that doesn't lie. So I became a special effects technician for film. I like nothing better than a good explosion, a successful conflagration. Of course, it's dangerous, but it's simpler than love isn't it?''

He thinks that is probably the reason behind all wars. She's lit up another cigarette after staring at the flame of her lighter a bit too long. From her left earlobe dangles a strange, scarlet-coloured leather earring shaped like a sardonic face.

''I've always lived alone. I built up a precarious little happiness, my heart well-protected behind barbed wire. I warmed myself on the false camaraderie of film sets, and my cat's affection seemed to be enough. I didn't feel much, except sometimes a fleeting tremor when I came upon lovers kissing on a street corner. I didn't even have nightmares anymore.''

''But why . . .''

''Love affairs gone bad, gone flat. Unfortunately I have little talent for forgetting and too great a talent for suffering.''

She falls silent. He'd like to reach out to her, comfort

her, breathe a little hope into her, but he doesn't find the right words. Resigned she shakes herself and says, "Come on, I can't take anymore of this noise."

She slips into her crimson coat, and without checking to see if he's following her, threads her way through the crude, raucous crowd. He catches up at the door and opens it for her with rather comical gallantry.

It is still raining, hard; she opens a large bright umbrella and they take refuge under it, elbow touching elbow. But with a continent between them.

She takes him down the street to the strange tear-shaped square below the rigid gaze of Norman Bethune. They sit down on a bench, both feeling the pitiless cold within more than the cold without. Again she's looked at her watch, and they stay like that, huddled together under the umbrella. Then she continues with what sounds like another sob in her voice.

"I first met him seven years ago, on a set. He's a cameraman. His wife is a make-up artist, aggressive and complaining. She didn't give him an inch; she was as jealous as a sick dog. I wanted to talk to him to find out at what distance he wanted to film a shack I was going to set fire to, but with her around, I couldn't get anywhere near him. I saw them again later, briefly, it's a small film crowd . . . I never spoke to him, even though I was burning to press him to me, naked. One of the last absolutes is fidelity, and respect for fidelity, don't you think?"

The man thinks like this stranger beside him. He's

totally against the fashion of "open" relationships, which seem to him just to be putting on a show of love. At this hour there are only occasional taxis prowling the asphalt mellowed by rain. Again he thinks about the woman he loves. Why is he so disturbed by this strange woman's affair? He doesn't want to miss a word of her story.

"In May this year when the weather was so mild, I was hired for a horror film called *The Journal of the Spider*. The ending required wonderful, bloody explosions that I was really looking forward to. I saw him arrive without his wife. He'd been hired with the second crew of special effects people. The way he looked at me! In his eyes I saw crazy hope, fear, and desire all mixed together. All day we worked side by side, each blushing every time we touched each other. And in the evening we went off to a bar and drank champagne till dawn. I thought love at first sight only happened in the movies. I was wrong."

In spite of her flamboyant umbrella the rain is running down her face. Again she looks at her watch. What is she waiting for? She continues, seemingly to herself.

"He hasn't lived with his wife for two years. I love him, but . . . his wife harasses us endlessly, phones in the middle of the night, dead drunk, threatens to kill herself, and each time he goes, just in case . . .I love him, I love him, but she makes it hell. I would love to reduce his past and mine to ashes, but that's impossible. The future is impossible. I can't take it any longer."

Suddenly a siren wails stridently from a neighbouring

street. Two fire trucks rush past blindly. The woman has looked at her watch again and she sights strangely before murmuring, "That isn't mine yet."

She has taken his hand. In the hollow of her palm, he can feel life beating, chaotically.

"And here's the weirdest thing. Three months ago I had to do some research for another film, *The Land that Forgets Itself*, which is set in 1931. So I went to the municipal library to read the magazines of that period; when I came to an ad for Knovak Salts at twenty cents a box, for fat people who suffer from the heat, a story came out of nowhere to haunt me, it was inexplicable, but it left me no rest. I had to write it down. The obsession deepened. I couldn't leave the house anymore; even at night I had to get up to correct a word, jot down a sentence. It got to be more unbearable than love, and so much more gripping."

Beside her, the man envies her this purpose, this creation that suddenly whisks away the banality of existence. He tells himself his life is empty because he has nothing like this, he has no art. The woman squeezes his hand harder. She's rivetted her gaze onto his, imploring him.

"I have the story with me. Do you have time to read it? I have twenty-five minutes left . . ."

Without waiting for his response, she digs around in her purple leather bag and hands him a wad of papers that have been folded and unfolded hundreds of times. He gives her the umbrella to hold, and she lights a cigarette. In the cold light of the street lamps he reads:

43

In spite of the great heat shimmering on the road, Jules Bigras was whistling for joy. He'd taken off the rough leather boots he made last winter and tied their laces together so he wouldn't wear them out, and they were bouncing around gaily on either side of his thick neck. He had at least another nine miles to go to the widow Ménard's house on the Crooked road in the village of Saintes-Plaies, but the crickets were singing, the late spring sun made him happy, and at the bottom of his pouch, right next to his little book on insects, nestled a bottle of homemade beer brewed from molasses. If it got too hot, he would have a drop, but only a drop. He didn't want to risk smelling like a drunk in front of the woman who was taking him on as a hired man.

He'd heard about the widow Ménard over secret drinks with two Czechs — Augustus Hoba, (nicknamed ''Smasher'' for his habit of breaking teeth when he was mad), and Steve Shoma (nicknamed ''Hunk-Nose'' because of the hard edges in his face). The men told him the widow Ménard was beautiful but chaste. And, particularly important during these Depression years — when you hired on for room and board and no salary — she was the best cook in the area.

Jules Bigras knew he would be sleeping in the stable, but the smell of hay and fresh manure was a thousand times better than the oily fumes from his tiny coal heater and the stench of his little tenement room in the city.

Thirty-seven years old, obese and limping, without a girlfriend, broke and still unemployed, Jules Bigras was whistling for joy on the gravel road to Saintes-Plaies.

The following Sunday around nine in the morning, Jules Bigras had already spent a good four hours digging the hole for the new outhouse, ten feet from the old one. The sun was pretty fierce for early June, but the earth offered him its comforting dampness and shadows.

A little way off, Gracia, widow Ménard's second daughter, eight years old with long brown braids, was exhibiting all the gravity of an orphan as she fed the white, black and grey chickens eagerly squawking about her.

Smiling, and dressed in the least-worn of her flowered muslin dresses, the widow leaned towards her hired man.

"Jules! Working on a Sunday! You're far too industrious! And you still haven't eaten have you?"

"Oh, Madame Ménard, seeing as this outhouse here is kind of urgent I thought I'd miss communion for once, so this morning at dawn I cut myself a piece of bacon and a crust of bread. But what's done is done, and if you happen to have any of last night's oatmeal left over, I wouldn't say no . . ."

Widow Ménard burst out in her charming laugh,

throwing back her head and shaking her blonde hair.

"Ah, it's a pleasure to see a man with an appetite! Come on, I'll heat it up for you."

An hour and a half later, after a bowl of porridge with maple sugar, after washing his neck at the pump and putting on his fresh shirt, after listening to the distressing account of how Monsieur Ménard drowned two winters ago, and after carrying four-year-old Candide, the youngest, on his shoulders all the way to the church three-quarters of a mile away, Jules Bigras did not enter the nave of the church. His excuse was that he had to put shoes on before he went into the holy place. He dilly-dallied with his laces until the carved wooden door closed on the last little believer. He waited until the children's choir entoned the first phrases of the introit, and then, as fast as his limp would let him, he headed for the cemetery at the far end of the village.

Jules Bigras leaned back against an old stone that no longer remembered its inscription. He took his small entomology book out of his pocket. He liked learning the names of insects: the Hop Merchant, the Once-Married Underwing, the Blind Sphinx. Then he thought about his wretched childhood and said to himself, "I am a free-thinker, I detest religion because of the cruel nuns in the Catholic orphanage." And then happily plunged back into the chapter on the Lepidoptera. At the end of the High Mass he raised his head, and it was just at that moment, at the dull chime of the single church bell, that he saw her for the first time.

With a net in her hand, she was chasing butterflies in the neighbouring field of public land. She was tiny, and wearing an old-fashioned black dress. Why didn't she have the same kind of flowery cotton dress the government gave to all poor women?

The woman felt someone watching her and raising her hand to her left cheek, she fled in the direction of the church.

That Sunday, June 1, 1931, under a sun that was the very image of hope, during High Mass at Saintes-Plaies, Jules Bigras fell in love.

Madame Ménard was in a bad mood on the way home. It wouldn't do for him not to go to Mass; it was sinful and she only hired good Catholics. Sinners could stand in soup kitchen lines in the city. Jules Bigras had to tell her all the details of his sufferings as a child in the orphanage before the widow took pity on him and forgave him. But he had to promise not to accompany her again to the village on a Sunday, so that the family's reputation would not be tarnished.

It wasn't until twilight on the following Wednesday that he dared ask about the woman who, like him, hadn't been to Mass.

Widow Ménard looked at him curiously. Had he asked his question in too detached a tone? Had his trembling hands betrayed him?

The butterfly woman was the curé's maid. People

only knew her first name, Malvina. She'd been left on the steps of the presbytery as a baby, about thirty years ago, and the good priest, Père Anthyme Chiasson, a young man at the time, had taken her in, raised her and, naturally enough taken her as a servant. People forgave her for not coming to Mass because they assumed she went to Matins or Vespers. And she never spoke to anyone, except a few words to Monsieur Rouleau, the owner of the general store, when she did her errands once a week. Widow Ménard concluded, "When you've got a birthmark that makes you look as though God hit you in the face, well, it doesn't lead to a lot of conversation."

Jules Bigras waited until late the following evening when everyone was asleep in bed to make his way to the presbytery.

The night was clear, warm, and fragrant, smelling of freshly-turned earth. He had to stop himself whistling for fear of attracting attention. He wanted to talk to Malvina, but hadn't the faintest idea how to go about it, though he was convinced he could make her happy.

He waited a while longer, his heart fluttering, until the village dogs grew quiet; then he approached the only lighted ground floor window at the back of the presbytery.

Holding his breath, he glanced into the small wood-panelled room, in the wavering light of the single oil lamp. There was Malvina, sitting at a rickety table and absorbed in a remarkable task. In front of her butterfly wings of various colours were arranged in different matchboxes. With a tiny pair of rusty tongs she selected a brown moth wing, brushed a spot of glue on it, and placed it delicately on a piece of canvas. She did the same with another wing.

Jules didn't move. His happiness was complete. From where he stood he could only see the right side of Malvina's face and he lost himself contemplating it. The more time that elapsed, the less he knew how he would approach her.

She finished her work and lifted it to examine it more closely under the lamplight. It was a portrait of an old Negro woman in tears. Malvina slowly pushed back her chair, closed the pot of glue, rinsed out the brush, carefully closed the matchboxes and put everything in the drawer of the table which she locked. With the picture under her arm she took a last glance around. Jules thought she had the look of a prisoner, but she saw him and wasn't afraid; she just leaned her head toward her shoulder to hide the birthmark. She seemed deathly tired. Malvina finally turned her back on Jules and with the lamp in her hand, she disappeared into the depths of the presbytery.

The whole next day, while he was doing the chores, and then while he was fixing the picket fence, Jules Bigras thought about the letter he would take to Malvina that evening. He so badly wanted to find the right words, the best words, that he didn't chat as he usually did with the widow, and he even got impatient with Eudoxie, the eldest, who was whining for him to patch up her doll's cradle.

In the evening this is what he wrote in his best hand:

Mademoiselle Malvina,

You don't know my name. I'm sorry I watched you working last night, but I couldn't help myself. You must forgive me. I wanted to meet you at any price and I was too shy to talk to you. I am thirty-seven, I limp, I am only a hired man, I am a little bit fat but in good health. If you like we could see each other.

I hope you will respond to my humble request,

Jules Bigras

On the way to the presbytery Jules feels extraordinarily jubilant. The walk seems so short, he even thinks he's stopped limping, and the plants, the wind and the moon are with him, even the frogs are croaking his love song.

Malvina has begun another picture with butterfly wings. Before he loses his nerve, Jules taps three times on the windowpane.

Dragging her feet and with her head down she goes to the window, half-opens it and bluntly asks, ''What do you want?''

Biting his lip, Jules hands her the folded sheet of paper.

She glances at it and gives it back to him, just as wearily. "I can't read. What do you want?"

He blushes, trembles, his hands are damp with sweat. He swallows hard, and finally says, "My name is Jules Bigras. I'm thirty-seven and . . . and I'd really like . . . to see you. If you like, if you'd let me, I'm sure I could teach you to read, I learned at the orphanage."

"That's not a bad idea. When?"

"I work all day at Madame Ménard's, so I could come in the evenings if you like."

"You'd have to hide, Monsieur le curé wouldn't like me to be seeing a man."

How much hatred there was in the three words "Monsieur le curé." It surprises Jules, but at the same time he is happy that he'll see Malvina again. He could have spent the rest of the night talking to her, but he hears steps inside the presbytery and only just has time to step aside.

When he dared look again, he saw the priest going off with his arm around his servant. Too familiar; much too familiar. Monsieur le curé Anthyme Chiasson was resting his hand on Malvina's behind.

The next day Jules Bigras took up his work at the farm with renewed vigour. The image of the curé's hand bothers him, but he is so happy that he manages to tuck it away into a compartment of his mind with everything else he wants to forget: his limp, the last two years of misery in the city, the suicide of one of the children in his class when he was little.

He has the energy of a torrent. He doesn't sleep much anymore because he spends a good part of his nights with Malvina in a forest clearing beyond the village green, amid the song of crickets and the fragrance of ferns. She always brings her oil lamp, paper and pencil, and he his book on entomology. She learns quickly and it's a pleasure to sit beside her, touch her with his elbow, guide her hand. Each time he loves her more and he wonders whether one day she will smile. He thinks that maybe the only way he can help her, or cheer her up is by marrying her. But when he knelt down in the grass in front of her one night in the full moon and stammered out his question, she turned frighteningly pale and ran off moaning.

All the next day Jules Bigras was afraid, more afraid than ever before that Malvina wouldn't come back to their meeting place in the clearing. He was so agitated he almost drove the axe into his good foot.

But Malvina was there, serious as a recent widow under the waning moon. She agreed to marry him, but here in the clearing, not at church, on Sunday in three weeks during High Mass. The wedding would be a secret, she said, and no one else would know about it. For the ceremony she would catch Harris' Checkerspot caterpillars on the asters in the presbytery garden, and elsewhere in the village if she had to. As soon as the larvae were rolled up in their cocoons Malvina would place them all around the clearing. Jules would have liked to understand the mystery of these wedding rites but Malvina refused to explain anything. Soon she was sobbing heavily and Jules was unable to console her under the powerless stars.

In the weeks that followed Jules Bigras saw the trees around the clearing draped one after the other in sheaths of white muslin. Little by little he became aware of the gigantic fairies concealed under their veils, watching over their love.

The Sunday dawned, shining with promise. As agreed, Jules didn't meet Malvina the previous night. He worked all Saturday evening twisting a thin iron wire into two wedding bands. He was not displeased with the result, though he deeply regretted being so poor that he couldn't buy beautiful rings of fine gold. He washed his best shirt, ironed it carefully and picked the prettiest flowers he could find.

Malvina arrived at the clearing before him. She was sitting in the tall grass. Her birth mark looks darker in the sunlight than it does at night. She has her precious butterfly wing pictures arranged around her.

Jules studies them one after the other, from the first ones where the design is awkward and uneven right to the last one of the old Negro woman. Her technique has been refined, the sadness is clearer. Always faces, faces of all racial types, in tears.

Malvina has meanwhile made a fire. With deliberation she takes her first picture and throws it into the flames. Jules wants to stop her, but Malvina sends him such a terrible glance that he is petrified, blocked. As she burns her life's work she finally tells her secret in a low voice.

"Monsieur le curé has looked after me all my life. He never taught me to read or write and he didn't want me to go to the local school; he'd say I should always, always stay with him. I was six years old when I started to scrub and polish, and eight when he showed me the kitchen. I never played with the village children because they made fun of my birthmark. I wasn't unhappy, I had enough to eat, and the sky is different every day. But when I was twelve, when I was twelve . . ."

She has covered her face with her hands and is trembling. Jules comes near her as gently as possible and touches her hair. The birds seem to grow silent, the crickets listen, and the breeze holds its breath. Malvina takes her hands from her face, then with her eyes looking straight into Jules's, she continues in a voice that is even more veiled.

"When I was twelve, on a Sunday, an hour before Mass, I remember it was snowing, everything was so white outside, so pure and still, Monsieur le curé came into my room. I was afraid, but I didn't know why. And then, and then . . . he took me. I closed my eyes. I wanted to throw up. And I wanted to die . . ."

Jules' blood boiled, anger suffocated him, pity drowned him. He held Malvina close, but she pulled away, more distant than winter. Now she's trampling her pictures before she throws them on the fire.

"Where could I have gone? Who would have believed me? It was the first time, only the first time. Monsieur le curé started again, at first only on Sundays, then every evening, before he read his breviary. It's as simple as that, my life ended one Sunday when I was twelve."

"Malvina, no, Malvina, we're going away together, right away, far away, we can be happy, I swear, I'll find a way for you to forget all that, you mustn't despair, I love you, and besides you had one little piece of luck in all your unhappiness, at least there was no child . . ."

She turned toward him, and he could hardly hear her voice.

"What do you mean? I am still a virgin. Monsieur le curé only ever took what he called "the back door"! No, it's no use, no use at all. I am dead, I have been dead for a long time already. I am sullied, forever sullied, and no one will ever be able to do anything for me."

The last picture is crackling in the fire. Jules has come close to Malvina. He's caressing her cheek, the one with the birthmark. He no longer sees the daylight, he no longer feels the soft glow of summer, his body isn't big enough for his heart which wants to burst. He pulls the two rings of iron wire out of his pocket and looks at them lying in his heavy hand, poor wedding bands for the poor, so pathetic, so useless.

"So why this ceremony, why the pupas in the trees?"

Malvina smiles, a miserable smile, but still her first smile.

"Jules, I can't offer you my life, because I have no life anymore. I can only ask you to die with me. That's all I have left, my death. But I'm afraid, all alone. Do you want to die with me?"

Malvina shows him two well-honed knives. Jules Bigras, his eyes moist, solemnly agrees. They exchange rings, and knives.

Together, they lift the muslin off the trees surrounding them, and standing close together at the centre of the clearing, they wait for the butterflies to dry their wings in the sun.

In their first kiss below the shimmering veil of a host of butterflies, Jules and Malvina die at each other's hands.

THE END

It's not raining anymore, how much time has gone by in this curiously-shaped square below the rigid gaze of Norman Bethune?

Why does the man shiver after he finishes reading the story? The answer he's been looking for for months is in his hands, luminous and terrible, in the tale of this absolute love.

He finally understands that the woman he loves doesn't love him, has never loved him. A flood of sadness breaks over him, but strangely, he is comforted by it, soothed. He raises his head, looks at the woman in red trembling beside him and reverently hands her the fifteen crumpled pages. Slowly he says, "You can love someone and die of it. Or love someone and live on. What about you?"

"You can love, and kill. What did you learn from my story?"

"That you mustn't love someone who doesn't love you. And what did you learn from writing it?"

She didn't reply, but suddenly got up and ran away. She crossed the street on a red light and a little further on plunged out of sight behind an old house wedged between two huge office buildings. He followed her but stopped at the entrance to the yard. He saw her break a cellar window and slither in through it like a snake.

An explosion resonated inside the house. A second-floor window blew out, then a tongue of flame leapt out and greedily climbed the facade. Cries sounded above the roar of the blaze. It seemed like an eternity but finally the ground floor door opened: wrapped in a quilt the arsonist appeared, coughing. She was carrying an unconscious woman with great difficulty.

Like an offering she placed the soft shape smelling of alcohol and smoke at the man's feet. Behind them, everything was in flames. A siren wailed in the distance.

"Who is it?," he demanded.

"The one who is truly loved by the man I love. Killing her would not have killed his love for her."

Before she disappeared she added, "The worst sentence is to live, not to die. Thank you for reading me. Unrequited love is only a needless fire."

PART II

demain montera de nouveau sur ses tréteaux
on tendra la main vers un ciel découvert

— Michel Beaulieu
FM, lettres des saisons III

Victim of the Shadows Where the Senses Meet the Heart

— Jean Cocteau

(Imaginary Journal, Fall 1986 — January 1988)

Why love at first sight rather than a tornado, an earthquake, or better yet a tidal wave? Nothing looks the same anymore, physical space is charged with fabulous signs, gems, fused gold, geysers tremble below the sidewalks, rubbies become prophets, everyone I used to know loses resonance, my tattered past suddenly smells of summer, of hot fruit pie, the pages of a new book, why you, why write you if not to make the moment of love discover its immortality, to ward off everything conspiring against us, our respective scars, the end of the millenium, the bombs and the evil, why write you if not to inscribe what is beating for you within me, my blood, my sex, my soul, and all my words are so small in relation to what moves me, like a child I repeat your name without believing in it, and I am so afraid but still I fear nothing, not even dying.

♦

By a strange set of circumstances that evening, a friend invited us to the theatre, and your former lover joined us. I didn't dare kiss you in front of her, but during the show I couldn't stop myself touching you lightly with my knee, slipping my hand under your belt, stealing glances at you, while the sad eyes of your former mistress robbed me of all my pleasure, my joy, my happiness at knowing your embrace, your smooth skin, your morning body all shaggy from the night, I would have wanted to seduce and love your former lover to console her for losing you, and suddenly I was suffering as though already you were moving away from me, as though the resonant temple of passion had brutally closed its doors on us, and later that night, after we'd come again and again and were motionless, listening to our hearts returning to their normal rhythms, and I was stroking your hair with the tips of my fingers in order never to forget it, I felt caught by the future, trapped in the immense and familiar grip of sadness, that you would leave me, later, tomorrow, always too soon, but I still thanked the goddesses of the present moment for you, there, next to me, with all my unarmed soul.

♦

As soon as you're gone, I cry from hunger; as soon as you're gone, the glowing coals that you lighted call for the hurricane of your kisses; as soon as you're gone, I rub my sex so that it exhales your most intimate juice; as soon as you're gone, I sleep or I write, I write you to dream you a little more; as soon as you're gone, my old terror of loving without being loved drains me, why, why, haven't we already snatched the purest essences from this bitter life, why, when as soon as you are here the spectres, the grey doubts disappear, why when as soon as you are here, with all the fragrant innocence of a first love, I savour your voice, the burn of your hand, why when as soon as you are here, I don't have enough for you in my two eyes, my two arms, my mouth, my sex and my heart?

◆

Suddenly, as though to find a better escape from suffering, the I fades away and the she arrives, suddenly she doubts what there is between them, she talks to him about it in a strangled voice, he reassures her and says, "I love you a lot" and suddenly this "a lot" seems inappropriate, and embarassing, and too small, and superfluous in his mouth, and she forgets the passionate gaze that later that evening he will have for her as he takes off her stockings, she forgets the kisses he will give her in his sleep, she forgets how he will silently rest his head on her belly as though in prayer, and in the morning, the warm toast he will bring her, even if she's said she's not hungry, but which she'll eat breathing in the happy fragrance of her body, she forgets to live what he gives her because she wants an impossible perfection from this love, almost ridiculous in this polluted era, and she finally understands that she'd either have to be the heroine of a novel, or dead, for this absolute to be appeased, and what good would that do her?

◆

Yesterday, as the storms you raised in my breathing were finally abating, as little by little the crackling of our kisses was dying out on our bodies, and the taste of the chocolate cake I baked us was clinging to our mouths, when with the abandon of a piece of human flotsam I was listening to your heart beat below your skin, the woman you loved so much, for such a long time, that woman, phoned with her poor little suicidal voice asking you to come running to help, and with the face of a condemned man you put on every piece of your clothing and you left, and I couldn't be angry with you, and especially not with her, because she's tearing herself apart for you just as I would tear myself apart, because she still loves you, maybe more and better than I do, and in this game of love and death the one who wins you loses you, and I'm not bitter at all, for with all the smiling fatality of a summer dawn spreading over the intimate catastrophes of our lives, the truth that you are mine and I am yours sings out to me.

♦

For the moment.

The light of another morning glistens in its golds and reds, again you came to see me, and joy flows through me like a virus, a drug, again you revealed the purest, the most perfumed water of your ruby body to me, and yet

♦

That was ten days ago. A week ago I phoned you because I couldn't bear just seeing you from time to time, late at night, when you had time. A week ago you told me, "I can't love you, you or anyone else." I said, "I'm stopping." You said, "I'll come see you. Later tonight." I said, "What for, what would we say that we don't already know?" You said, "I'll phone you." I said, "Well, I won't phone you. You can't be my friend. I don't want that." I can't anymore. Already. I said, "I'm stopping." I don't have the patience to wait for you to love me one day. Too worn-out. I said, "No, I won't be calling you." I've been lying for seven days. And seven nights. I do phone you. Every day. Every night. As soon as I hear your voice, I hang up. Your voice is smooth. Even happy. I don't have a voice left. From crying too much. From lamenting. From being betrayed. Apparently you don't remember. You've been lying too. For seven days. For seven nights. I said, "I'm stopping." One day you told me, "I've decided not to suffer anymore." It's as if you told me I decided not to live anymore. It's true, you don't feel pain anymore. You don't feel joy. You don't feel life. You only have a vague memory of soft abandonment. Of the exquisite vulnerability of love. Sometimes a wisp of nostalgia must break through that lovely wall in you, for the small space of an instant. I write, I still write you so that chink may one day widen into the sea.

♦

Then you disappeared. That was five months ago. I made my girlfriends laugh when I nicknamed you "Six weeks," or "Sudden disappearance," and I hated you for not giving me a sign, as though nothing, nothing had burgeoned between us. Bitterly I congratulated myself for feeling more alone with you than without you, and then even your memory dissipated, as it grows older the heart considers its new wounds more philosophically, but in May, with May, you came back to me, in the soft air that smells of rutting and cries of kissing, trembling that I didn't want you anymore, but I did, and I abandoned myself again, forgetting nothing, I can't forget anything anymore, and I'm still lying as I write because I had forgotten, for the sake of my survival, how much I liked sleeping with you, and talking, the other night how I almost fainted from climaxing and thought I'd die, you stroked my hair and talked about buccaneers and then about dinosaurs, and I was naked on your nakedness, and those words between us that soothed me, and a few days later when I was trying to sketch you from memory, and couldn't remember the shape of your eyebrows, no, no, I forget everything except the suffering from your absence and that's not true either because I'm always laughing with you, I always come with you, and I don't dare admit to myself that I love you, except here, in the secret of an electronic memory, and since I see how easily I forget, I'm trying to fix the other moment here, later still, when you have left my bed and the whole spark of your happiness has pierced my soul, and like a litany

I repeat the smile you had a few nights ago, the shape of your lips after your kisses, last autumn I didn't know how to love you, I didn't know how to love because I wanted guarantees, as though you were a car, or a curling iron, to feel the true savour of love and the bite of life, there is only the instant, the instant to be devoured, and you are here, with me, thank you, thank you life.

♦

Here I am with the eye of a microbiologist, and the meticulousness of a hagiographer, here I am scrutinizing the least of your expressions, playing back the least of your inflections, the sound of your voice when you said my name yesterday, the velour of your voice when we're alone, and peaceful, but also that sardonic light in your eyes when at night you will not rest until I have come and come, from the wall to the bed to the floor to the front room, standing, lying, turned over, open, tucked up, come and come again until I've lost my identity, until I become one with every female in heat, from the whale to the bitch, and you endlessly hold back your ejaculation, and tell me it's a mystery to you, this infinite retention, this pleasure you constantly defer without losing an iota of your erection, and you pull me close, and say, "Put your arms around my neck," and you carry me, more liquid than the sea, to the turbulent sheets, I am so tremulous from orgasm that I can't take a step, and you whisper that it's a mystery to you, because it only happens with me, with me alone, and that you love seeing me come and come, and in vain I feel my skin grow vast as a continent, I too want and love to see you come, see your face find its original earthen shape, this collapse that is the most suave of all the cataclysms, oh my lover, what beautiful vengeance I am preparing, how impossible will be your escape.

♦

You're the one who first talked about a little fishing trip together, I hope I didn't give myself away, I hope my joy kept quiet; to spend forty-eight hours with you, so many seconds of happiness, watch you awaken on two mornings, would my impoverished soul withstand such exhilaration, and I talk about all this as though it were difficult when it is a question of happiness, have I lived so long in the stench of wounds that the fragrance of flowers frightens me?

◆

I grow weary writing you, how can I render the thousand nuances of joy, could it be that the suffering within me finds more words than the joy? And if I talk more about the loving of our bodies it is because of their sheen, my brutality according you savagery, your tenderness setting free my gentleness, I can hardly resist covering your skin with the marks of my nails, my teeth, if I could tattoo you I would not shrink from writing my name on you ten thousand times.

♦

Does he love me, does he love me, or am I just a part of his routine, is he with me only for the cries of ecstasy he can extract, where is the truth, where is the trauma, damned chaos of endless questions. Today I feel only like dying, today death has more logic, more flavour than life.

♦

What am I complaining about? Why am I complaining? Aren't you my only wealth, my only bulwark against the void. Still this anguish, thinking that it's just your nature, that you're like this with me and with all the others, the other women, so tender, that it's only your fear of being alone that attaches you to me, four months now I've spent with you, and you haven't said you love me, and you know the value of words, if you don't utter them you don't feel them, I haven't said anything either, but I write it, I write it to you without you reading it, in any case I almost have to twist your arm to make you read me. But what if the love I write means more to me than reality? And what if this silence aerates my blood, a unique way of subsisting? But your soul isn't free, not yet, I am only your respite, your refuge, maybe I should leave you, what have I got to do with the gentleness of living, with compromises, why can't I revel in you at any hour of the day and the night, why not at every minute, why are you still so preoccupied with the woman you once loved and love no longer, why do you want to console what can't be consoled, I have the feeling I'm spoiling my tiny chances at happiness by letting you leave at any hour of the night to save her, while I get lost in the quicksands of patience, so alone, can't I survive without you, is my only strength the strength to wait for you?

I hate this century of steel hearts, so often wounded they can only palpitate behind their walls of reinforced concrete, and only faintly, and without resonance.

♦

I told you on the phone that I was getting depressed and you came by quickly at lunch with salads and wine, to make me eat, but I couldn't swallow anything because my soul was knotted with anxieties and I told you everything, that I loved you, that I was afraid, that I couldn't bear these midnight calls anymore from the woman you once loved, that I was thinking of leaving you, and you reassured me, and now that you've gone, I laugh at myself, you came back with the night, and caressed me the way you did when you hardly knew me, and bit into my neck, and entered me with the secret savagery I find so moving, and I was nothing but this immense flower chalice that opens between my legs, inundated with joy and juices, more aromatic than the jungle, more turbulent than a galaxy.

♦

Yesterday as we were falling asleep, you whispered, "Forgive me for being fat, forgive me for only coming to eat and sleep." Sweetheart, I love your extra kilos, they are touching signs of gluttony, and if you eat here it's because I love concocting delicacies for you, and I love sleeping bonded to you, with your arms and legs clasping me so tightly that death could overtake us and I wouldn't be afraid, I love you for everything you are that I know, everything you are that I don't know, and so you may as well forgive me for never wanting to eat, for being obsessive, for not sleeping with you or drawing your white essence from you more often, though I love to make you moan, but life offers so much to discover and to try, I love being tired with you from our days, from having laughed and talked too much, go to sleep, sweet love, every second carries its burden of sparks.

♦

You rented a cottage for me for two days and three nights at the edge of a lake in the luxuriance of autumn, and on the first night you fell asleep on the sofa, while I, stretched out between your legs with my head on your belly, remained motionless so as not to disturb your sleep, and when I did have to get up you awoke in such confusion, with so much sadness in your eyes, and you grabbed hold of me, caressed me and fucked me so furiously, almost despairingly, I thought that night I would disintegrate, and I cried for a long time, because you opened the door to the enclave where I had concealed all my pain, and it surged through my soul with all its suppressed force, here I am truly naked, without my armour, so vulnerable with my organs and my flesh open to the quick, my hardened shell split open and destroyed, there, now I won't be able to defend myself anymore, I've lost all my secrets, I forgive everything, I forgive myself everything, I forgive myself all my men, be careful now of every move, of every word, each one will lodge in my rawest essence.

♦

Every time she's in love she gets her hair cut very short, like a boy's, so that her femininity is hidden even more from everyone but him alone, so that she can't hide her face from the man she loves, but if she is happy, why does she have so little energy, why does she only want to sleep, why can she only write platitudes, and with such difficulty? She knows only thirst, this love does not quench it, she knows only its idolatry, it seems that her heart could find total peace by endless contemplation of the one she loves, winter's coming, she wished they'd never had to leave the watery depths where last summer they held hands, marvelling at the shape of algae, as overhead the sun accomplished miracles, she would like everything living around them to die, so that they might recreate a new ordering, more tender, without a single demand, or misfortune, or power struggle of any kind, a universe of kisses and laughter, a civilization of benign gratification, doesn't she feel reality wearing down her love for him, drop by drop, death catching up to shake her and howl, and nothing, nothing, nothing able to save her?

◆

Each time she wants to withdraw from him, and find the illusory quiet of her solitude, he surrounds her with so much tenderness that she's misled for the moment, she misconstrues, she refuses momentarily to look her truth in the eyes, it is only afterwards when she's alone that she can think clearly and tell herself: I have to get away, I have to leave him, as long as he's preoccupied by the one he loved before me, there is no space in him for me, I want a man with inner spheres clear of all nostalgia, of all remorse, I'm leaving you, love, with so much sadness, thank you for everything I lived with you, but it is still not enough, I prefer to free myself from you while I am still able, other men will come to me whom I will love even more and who will love me too, and if no one comes, I will respect this absolute ideal that is essential to me, more essential than love, and I will survive.

♦

Once again she left him for good, she held out four days and three nights contemplating her heart's disaster, then she cracked again, saw him again, he had all the good arguments, she doesn't know anything anymore, isn't sure of anything, all she knows is the fleeting scent of happiness on certain evenings when she can be with him, so is there nothing else for her but this brief and tenuous fragrance, is that how it is now for every man, every woman, this moment of joy always too short? Is there nothing more than words to prolong happiness?? Only words and their burden of solitude???

She is tortured. Distress, such distress. She is mired in what seems a stinking mud of unexpressed lies. By accident — but is it really an accident? — she gets pregnant, sobs for days, begs him, questions him about his love for her, about the truth of his love for her. In the end he admits he doesn't love her, never loved her, will never love her. Finally relieved, finally soothed, she breaks with him forever. Then she aborts what was growing inside her, her love for him, of him.

♦

Everything has become clear. It doesn't matter who or when I love. I see that love's assassin is hidden away within me, with his sweaty fears, his breath reeking of lies, his pallid despair. It doesn't matter who or when I love. I will have to fight off the killer to the end.

♦

Aléa

The First Night

I've just finished a six-month gig at home, with six shows a week and a daily audience of five thousand: people reaching for me, calling for me, applauding me. So much love is murderous. Here, I'm far away from all that, it's quieter, much colder, I mean the temperature — it's like a prison camp in Siberia and I only have my old felt hat against all this wind, all this white. I'm here for six nights, eight hundred people an evening. Why am I here, really, what am I running after? Do I still have the choice, any choice?

I go into the Spectre — this is my stage, my arena — and they point out a woman leaning against the wall who's been waiting for me for two hours already, a tiny shadow, without a coat, red-headed. I like redheads. I go up to her. She's wearing shoes that look like two moonless summer nights starred with gold. How did she avoid getting them wet with all this snow everywhere? Did she fly here? Closer. Suddenly there's a spring murmuring in my head, as though it wanted to escape toward the light.

"I am Ada Lazuli. Here, this is from a friend. I owe her a lot."

Seldom seen eyes like that, sharp blue, with a fleck of laughter floating in their depths. She gives me a black velvet box with more golden stars that looks as if it belongs to a second-rate magician.

"From a friend? Who's that?"

"Look out, it's fragile."

"What do you owe her?"

She hesitates as though she were about to rip open a mystery. I say nothing. Barely a whisper comes from Ada Lazuli.

"Imagine a desert, and suddenly a gust of rain out of nowhere that leaves behind an oasis and cactus flowers like soft daggers . . . you understand?"

"I think so. I don't know. Listen, I'm really late, they're waiting for me. I've got a new synthesizer and we have to do the sound balance . . ."

In the filthy dressing room, I take the lid off the box, and a grey dove escapes, flutters about, perches on my shoulder, and pecks my ear. I laugh; no one ever thought of that one before. The bird lands among the pots of make-up. A thin cylinder of engraved silver is attached to its claw.

An answer or a question?

First I extract a fine strand of black hair, at least a meter long, tied with a purple ribbon, then a sinsemilla flower that is also almost purple, and finally a tiny piece of folded paper, crowded with rounded letters in a slanting hand:

Hedgehog, will you come see me? Let Plunderer go.
                                                    Aléa

Plunderer? Aléa? A token? A game?

Hedgehog? How could anyone know that? My friend in Berlin nicknamed me Hedgehog fifteen years ago in Barcelona, just before he died. Who? And how?

In answer to Aléa's note, I tear the edge off a magazine lying on the floor, and write, "Don't know." I enclose my message in the silver cylinder. Plunderer is nervous, but holds still. I take the dove, his heart beating in my palm, and release him through the fire exit. He disappears into the storm.

I close the door. I smell the black strand of hair. It was cut today and still gives off scents of ambergris and cypress with a hint of bitterness I can't identify.

Is it a supple necklace or a hangman's rope? I wrap the long strands around my neck. This evening, I will inhale its delicate fragrance each time I lean into the mike.

The Second Day

I'm hardly awake. I touch my throat. The necklace has vanished. I want to retain the sands of my dreams, but with eyes half-closed I shuffle off to the first interview of the day.

What is it about green steel that they like so much,

green metal for the interior of bars. Here and in Paris; it's enough to make you puke. The neo-punk reporter across from me, with his nice carnivore's head, isn't crazy, no, he's honest, sincere, friendly. I like it when they want to shoot the breeze with me.

As he leaves the journalist hands me a book. Signed by Aléa, it's called *Moist Montreal*.

"Why are you giving me this?"

"No reason."

"Do you know her?"

The neo-punk smiles, revealing his sharp canines.

"Do you ever know anyone?"

"Sometimes, yes. For an instant."

"That's it. Let's just say that she led me out of the darkness."

"She wants to meet me."

"That's delicate. Careful."

Then the wolf turned his back on me as though he'd said too much. The bar has emptied, the greenness starts murmuring like flowing water. I turn the pages. In the margins are drawings of miniature couples in obscene poses. It's a collection of stories, too violent, too raw, desperate. Not my kind of reading.

It tugs at the scars, inside.

The Third Night

There's a party after the show.

For me.

At the top of a staircase with forty-six steps.

In the club above the Spectre.

The Russian Roulette.

Where I sang.

Ten years ago.

I dragged myself up the forty-six steps.

The neon lights are flickering.

I don't hear anyone.

I'm exhausted.

Damn! Another journalist.

Luckily she's not ugly.

Right, let's do the tightrope number.

Get it over with.

I'm wasted.

Finally, I can't stop myself, I can't help asking, "Who is Aléa?"

The girl has started panting. She looks as if she's just got on a motorcycle that was moving at top speed.

"Aléa? They think she's the same woman who signed her name to the ten most pornographic films made in the States; here she's been churning out horror stories to fill the racks. Over the past five years every one of our magazines has had its own little controversy over her filth. And this is a small country, so everything gets out; we media at least know that she supplies eminent politicians and famous artists with drugs, and that means anything — powders, roots, leaves, charms, potions . . ."

"That's not what I want to know. What's she like?"

"I've never seen her. I'm looking for her. But . . ."

She throws me a glance that is probably just as pointed as her pen. I don't like it. But I don't have much choice.

"What else?"

"I'm only telling you this because of who you are: five years ago, after your opening at the Grand Dérangement, a minor actress had a fight with her lover, a pathetic, unknown musician. I was there. It was quite something. She wanted to meet you in your dressing room and he didn't want her to. They had a real scuffle and she ended up rushing outside where she was run over by a car. And he's never been seen again."

There's the roaring of a river, a disaster crashing in on all sides. I have to hold on to the thread, no matter how slimy.

"What's the connection with Aléa?"

"At the time the actress had hair down to her ass. That's all I know. It's no proof. Just a suspicion. Why are you so interested?"

"No reason. Don't know."

Why should I nourish a viper?

The Fourth Night

I emerge from the Spectre at two o'clock in the morning. In the street a howling white squall is sculpting ephemeral phantoms. Right in front of me there's a van painted with fleshy ferns, a thicket of mangrove and Mbura trees — it could have been painted by Le Douanier Rousseau, a tropical oasis in the middle of winter. Suddenly, a woman wrapped in blue furs calls out, "Hedgehog?"

Shit. Someone else who knows. It's incredible. Does every secret have holes in its pockets over here?

She gives me a smile that would send me to hell if I weren't already there.

"Did Aléa send you?"

"Yes, I'm Jeanne Couteau, a friend of hers. She just said I had to contact you. Get inside."

She slides the door open and climbs in after me. It's like in *A Thousand-and-One Nights*, all richly-coloured rugs, and embroidered cushions. I stretch out. It's soft, silky, and torrid. The woman knocks on the glass separating us from the driver, and Baghdad sets off. Where to?

"Is this Aléa's van?"

"Yes, but she never goes out."

"What does she want with me?"

"That's up to you. Be careful."

Jeanne Couteau kneels down at my feet. She's undone her furs and her fair skin gleams underneath. She removes my heavy boots and my socks, and strokes my ankles with her plump hands.

"I'm thirsty."

"There's some champagne in a bucket behind you and an engraved silver flute glass."

I take a drink. I feel as though I'm in the centre of a torrent and stop Jeanne Couteau who's already caressing my thighs.

"Why are you supposed to contact me?"

"She never explains. It's all so delicate."

Jeanne Couteau reaches for me greedily, her succubine lips all over my face, but I don't want to kiss her, I want to know.

"Who is Aléa, though?"

Jeanne Couteau pulls back to size me up. Her name is appropriate. She presses back against me and her sharp, child-like voice rises like a mist.

"All I can say is that I was angry. Ever since I was capable of love. That's a long time. Rage toughened me up. My skin was coated with basalt reinforced with steel, so airtight it was killing me. Then I met Aléa, and it all crumbled. Understand?"

Jeanne Couteau's eyes well up. I'm pretty tough but when I'm moved I give in.

"I want to see her."

As though he's heard every word I said, the invisible driver abruptly changes course.

She takes me to the west end — the English part of town. We enter a high-rise where an aged doorman, limping horribly, opens the door after he gives Jeanne a conniving glance. In silence we take the elevator to the thirtieth floor. Oh I'm slipping along a cliff, a waterfall is carrying me along, deafening me.

Then we turn left, pass through a metal door, climb two sets of stairs and emerge on the roof. There's no sign of footsteps. At this height the wind is howling from the very depths of the Arctic.

Jeanne Couteau points northward.

"You want to see her? Come over to the edge and look down. When you're really ready to meet her, she'll arrange it."

The air turns gentle as a kiss and just as heady. Twenty-seven stories below us a blue rectangle stands out in the night, the translucid roof of a swimming pool; slowly a woman with hair down to her feet slips through the water without disturbing the surface. Aléa turns on her back and greets me with a gesture of her arms. Why suddenly this pain inside, this gangrene of sadness. Why this deathly ache? And why suddenly all this snow rushing down from above — why does the ragged sky choose this very moment to hide Aléa from me? Why?

The Fifth Night

No message from Aléa today, neither before nor after my show. I stayed at the bar of the Spectre as long as I could. I listened to my fans stammer out their homage; I waited for a sign that never appeared.

A little drunk, I returned to the hotel, to my beige room, and collapsed on my drab bed.

Under my pillow I discover a black mink schapska. I try it on and am submerged in ambergris and cypress with that hint of bitterness I still can't identify. I give up. But how can I reach her in the middle of the night? I grab for the telephone. I haven't dialed her number, I haven't even heard the dial tone, before a low female voice says, ''Yes?''

I take a deep breath before I leap into the abyss. Taking a chance, I say, ''I want to meet Aléa.''

''I am Aléa, Come, the doorman will let you in.''

''It's not too late?''

''I never sleep. The vigilant don't sleep.''

''But I'm tired too.''

"So much the better — I'm sixty-thousand years old today."

Did I really leave the hotel; throw myself into the taxi that seemed to be waiting for me, and without saying a word, arrive back at the high-rise?

The old, lame man released the bolt on an elevator I hadn't noticed the last time, and as the gate closed, he said, "Careful with Aléa."

Careful because she's delicate, or because she's dangerous? The mahagony elevator moves up to the twenty-ninth floor. Here I am at the door. My head is spinning; it's the beer I drank much earlier. I tell myself life is short, there's no point hesitating. When someone pursues me insistently, I always end up giving in. I'm too much of a gentleman.

I hear, "Come in, Hedgehog," in that strange, low, tremulous voice. And so I go inside. As though I were in the airlock of a submarine, I take off the schapska, the heavy boots, the thin gloves, my silk scarf, the unlined coat, my cotton sweater. The vestibule already makes me uncomfortable: dozens of dolls are hanging from the walls, observing me with their glass eyes; a red rope ladder is suspended parallel to the ceiling; and three grey cats are watching me. Again Aléa's voice calls out, "Charade, Chagrin, Heatwave, bring him in to me."

Finally, there she is in front of me lying on a chaise-longue in a room that is completely blue, wearing mauve silk pyjamas with her hair flowing down to the floor. Never have I seen eyes so dark, so weary. Here too there are rope ladders on the ceiling. Charade is playing with the tip of Aléa's hair. Heatwave has dozed off. Chagrin is licking her chops.

"So you're the one who's been sending me all those messengers? Why? Who are you?"

She's silent, smiles, lights a cigarette. She looks about thirty. With a beating heart, I say, "I'm all dressed up. Can we have some light?"

She snaps her fingers and three candles light up. I feel hungry, and with a gesture graceful as a wave, she shows me the kitchen. A tray seems to be waiting for me, with champagne, caviar, fruits, chocolate. I bring it in, I've never been so hungry. I sit down at her feet. I devour everything: the chocolate of my childhood, the peaches that have the exact smell of the first girl I ever made love with, the true sweet and sour caviar of my first successes. What a sorceress! How could she have known all that? She's smoked six more cigarettes; she's still not talking. I take her hands, so moist and cool, rest my head close to her; a wash of ambergris and cypress anoints me. Again I ask, "Who are you?"

"Everything you've heard about me is true, and false. Watch."

She sends a puff of grey smoke over towards the big window. As in the cinema, a flock of clouds rush across the space and bursts into downy snow.

And as though that weren't enough, the sparkling chiffon of an aurora borealis ripples through.

Then everything disappears. Just as before, the city spreads out its electric jewels at our feet.

93

I am breathless and say nothing.

Aléa murmurs, "That isn't me. It's a power, one of my powers. It's chance. I am chance."

"But can you do everything? Guess everything? Know everything?"

"No, I never know what you will choose."

"And why do your friends love you so much?"

"My friends? I am a rocky desert in the darkness. I just crossed their paths. I made only one gesture toward them and they thought they knew me, they thought I helped them. They're wrong. They helped themselves."

"And me, why me?"

Chagrin is playing with the tip of her hair. Charade has dozed off. Heatwave is licking her chops. Aléa finally bursts out, "There are souls at peace, and souls at war, and I find the latter more amusing."

"But what do you want from me?"

She doesn't open her lips except to smile. Her face looks like a little girl's in front of a wrapped present. I get up and say, "Come on, what else is there except kisses and caresses?"

I go into the pink room ahead of her and turn around. She's followed me effortlessly, gripping the crossbars in the rope ladders. She can't walk. She embraces me, whispering, "There are deities left, a few devils, and words. Hold me tight or I'll collapse."

I grit my teeth: deities — the very idea is repugnant, it stops me breathing, but she was about to fall, so I held her close. I had to carry her to the bed. I helped her off with her jacket. She has fine, white skin but a monstrous upper body with over-developed shoulders and a wrestler's biceps. She wants to encircle me with the powerful chain of her arms but I disengage myself roughly. This whole business is already far too tempting; damn the tenderness. Without the slightest embarassment she crosses her wrists behind her and says, "Pull off my pants."

I retort, "No orders, don't give me orders!"

Without losing her child-like smile, she replies, "Can't I give orders? Or can I just beg for favours?"

And she opens her fleshless legs, which are too long, and dead. It's like when I play certain chords on my old piano and can't resist the vibration. I move my hands over her pale breasts, caress her scrawny hips. She undulates like a scorpionfish in a fountain of sighs and suddenly I seize her throat, press down, and yell, "Come, or I'll kill you!"

Why do I do that, if not to exorcize this squalid fear of being disarmed, made vulnerable, pierced through? I want to destroy a goddess, I want to reduce her to nothing, less than nothing. I'm really strangling her and across her face pass lightning waves of youth and old age until she finally covers her eyes. But she's laughing, laughing! I leap back, shouting, "Who are you making fun of?"

She replies in a languid voice, "Look at me. How could I make fun of anyone?"

With her hair dishevelled she looks like a siren washed ashore in a shipwreck by a hurricane. She adds, "For a moment I was afraid of death. I thank you for that. The fear of death is so sweet, so precious, so rare . . . But then I panicked for you. I would have crushed you with one blow. You would have died before me, because, you see, I can't.''

She takes a carafe of water from a low table and drinks from the spout. I understand less and less. The surf is washing over me. She says, ''I settled here because living in a land of agony is like living at the heart of an orchid that will never open.''

''But why is your body like that?''

''We don't have a choice. Never. When we want to be incarnated we take the first available body, the one that is dying at that very instant. I found myself with this one.''

I stretch out on my back beside her, I spread out my arms and demand, ''Caress me.''

She doesn't move, but continues, ''If I touch you I will freeze you. Sixty-thousand years of dust and solitude are too cold for you. I chose you because you move me, you amuse me with your dreams. When will you know that only the moment counts, only the moment that is so delicate. That's all you've been given, and if you breathe it in you will perhaps be able to pick up the frail scent of happiness.''

She has grown quiet. It's a pretty full silence. Heatwave is playing with the tip of her hair. Charade has dozed off. Chagrin is licking her chops. I am just listening to my blood sprinting from my head to my sex to my heart.

I give in. Very slowly I let my body slip full length

over her, I touch her moist eyelids and my erection presses close against her, so fragrant and glistening with succulence, so near her that I feel her vulva quivering. She's chanting now in Iroquois, or Babylonian, a rapid guttural song, hypnotic and thousands of ages old. I understand nothing but I know she's calling me, against my glans her other lips are stammering out the same chant, it could drive me mad or to my death, as though I were foundering at the centre of an abyss. I'm no longer afraid of anything, not even of drowning. I feel I could dive right through to the next continent, lose myself and yet gain enormous strength, but a strand of Aléa's hair wraps itself around my foot and holds me back. I implore. I beseech, ''Do you want to? do you want to?'' and as she continues to laugh, I free myself and finally enter her.

Charade is playing with the tip of her hair. Chagrin has dozed off. Heatwave is licking her chops. Later, much later I fell asleep on the chaise-longue, then later still, the sun hadn't yet risen completely, Plunderer cooed from somewhere, and I called, ''Aléa!?''

She was up against the big window, suspended by one hand, completely focused on the clouds, as attentive as though she were silently speaking for the defence. Without a glance at me she said, ''It's only from here, from down below, that the sky is so beautiful. From above, it's a dismal horror. Do you want to make a wish?''

I stammered, ''I'd like to have my old Pleyel with me tonight,'' and she laughed again, as though it were nothing at all, such a heavy piano, so fragile and so forgotten on the other side of the Atlantic.

The Sixth Night

"That evening, you made your choice. You came on stage carrying me in your arms. You placed me like a cut flower on your old grand piano. You sang with a new break in your voice, in your soul, in your heart. Finally, you had an echo. Have you fully understood its magnitude?"

Psyche from Here

I remember exactly how everything started. It was a
night in the middle of March, glacial and moonless;
nonetheless I was naked, curled up under my electric
blanket set at maximum heat. I had the impression my
bones would never be free of winter.

I wasn't sleeping. I wasn't even trying. To tell the
truth I surrendered to insomnia ages ago (in this
tormented world I can't help but keep my eyes open,
it's a question of anxiety). That week it was the five
thousand corpses done in by mustard gas in the city of
Halabja that were keeping me going. Setting me off.

My next door neighbour was listening over and over
again to that song of Corey Hart's: "I wear my
sunglasses at night, so I can, so I can . . . ." Later I
got to thinking that the whole universe was conspiring
against me that night.

It all started like this. I felt a length of warm fur
tremble along the tips of my fingers on my left hand. I
shivered. It didn't feel at all like Chansonette's, my grey
cheviot cat. It bore a terrible resemblance to a man's

hair, both thick and fine! My heart pounding, I turned on my amaranth lamp and lowered my only defence against calamity, but there was nothing under the wrinkled sheets, nothing at all!

And no person either!!!!

I was beginning to assume I was having a postdated hallucination from my only acid trip (ten years ago), when I noticed Chansonette in a crouching position, two meters away.

Her gaze was rivetted on a corner of the room, a completely uninteresting corner cluttered with old shoes: her pupils wide, she was staring at a precise point in space, at about the height of a man.

Yes, of a man.

Then, just as she does when you stroke her, Chansonette lowered her head and closed her eyes, and I even heard her purr particularly loudly. She went so far as to lie down on the cold floor, completely displaying herself, stretching up her little underbelly for a caress, an obscene little kittenish trick that she has always reserved exclusively for me. Always, just for me . . .

It should have sent cold chills down my back, but I blushed as though in front of a fire.

◆

The next day it rained. When I began to get drowsy around the same hollow hour I took some precautions. If I held my breath for just a moment I would have fallen asleep. So I didn't bother turning off the television. I had pirate cable channels, and with the music station on, submerged in the trembling light of a Pierre Flynn clip, I had a vague impression that these lines were endlessly streaming by: ''Searching through the broken nights of capital cities, I followed her and lost her so many times.'' But I'm not totally sure of that since my memory, finally grown quiet, also dozed off.

Around five in the morning an electrical failure woke me up. Or to put it more accurately, I was shaken by the sudden silence. No more rock music, no more rattling humidifier, nothing. Curiously, it smelt of grass after a rain, but also of summer sand, and when I concentrated hard enough, I picked up the sweet scent of hyacinths. I saw nothing but Chansonette's eyes glowing in the crime-black room.

Then I heard my pussy-cat let out a little cooing sound. I guessed she was languishing in that uninteresting corner, and if I let out a moan, it was not from fear, but from desire. Hermits must feel the same way when an inspiration draws them forth.

As though to avoid frightening me, someone lightly touched my hair, then an imperceptible but delicious kiss was placed on my shoulder, and I had the flavours of a feast in my mouth, or more precisely, a mouthful of Ouzo first, then some ripe, black olives, bursting with sun, and then goat cheese flavoured with basil and a trickle of olive oil, and finally a delicate sweet of honey and puff pastry.

When I felt a man's feverish and angular hand (yes, a man's hand) on my belly, and especially when I felt someone slowly nibble the nape of my neck — which electrified me right down to my toes and soaked me between my legs — it was irresistible, I couldn't hold back, I wanted to see this exquisite intruder who knew me so well. I picked up my lighter from the bedside table and lit it.

My bed and my room were just as empty as my heart.

Chansonette eyed me scornfully, as though I had ignored a painfully obvious detail.

There was a tearing inside me.

◆

The next day I understood. That night I closed the coral blinds as a reddish moon was rising, I put on clean sheets that smelled of hope, and I perfumed myself a little too much (as I always do when I have a date).

Still naked, I stretched out, more ardent and tremulous than the noon-day heat on the road.

Chansonette was at her post in the corner that was now beginning to become interesting. I waited, and waited, I was absolutely patient, but it wasn't until an hour before dawn that a distant and indolent chant began slowly moving toward me, with its ancient harmonies of sistrum and lute. As a further precaution, I closed my eyes and had a vision of a host of sprites dressed in madder and absinth-coloured muslin forming a smiling ring around me.

The same stranger lay down at my side. I felt his erect penis against my hip, its satiny pulsations, and I felt faint. I didn't move for fear that the charm be broken. His hand wandered over my entire body as though to awaken the blood, but there was no need: my heart was battering me to the breaking point; the stranger was quivering too, his knee opened mine, his lips opened mine, I imbibed his sweet saliva, our breathing harmonized like an orchestra, the grain of his skin is smooth as youth, his chest teases my nipples, his navel touches mine, his palms meet mine, and he slips into the ravine between my thighs, he grasps the knot of my desire with his breath, his mouth, his tongue, with all his soul. As I ascended the spiral of sensuality my last lucid thought was that only a god unaware of any form of violence could love me so well.

When I awoke, dawn was cutting its blonde light into the coral blind and my room was still swaying in the fragrant murmurs of the sea.

◆

Later that day, I decided on an experiment.

Spring was streaming in, blushing at its belated arrival. At noon, the sun came showering down, the air was dancing, drunk with heat, and motorcycles were criss-crossing like mysterious flaming swallows.

I locked myself into my windowless bathroom. Chansonette was rolled up in the sink, as was her daytime habit. I bolted the door, just in case. It was pitch dark. I started filling the bathtub with water and groped for a sachet of dried flowers and two handfuls of coarse salt to soften the skin, which I added. I lowered myself into the hot water. To be on the safe side, I closed my eyes. Would he come?

My right hand was dangling over the steamy edge of the tub. A cooing sound from Chansonette was the first sign. Then, just as happily, the chant of the night before drew near with the step of a gentle doe; delicate fragrances of seaweed tinged with orange coiled around me, and a fleeting breeze touched my wrist like a fuchsia petal.

Before I melted into the euphoria of his presence, I breathed: ''Who are you?''

He held me close and enchanting zephyrs raised us into the atmosphere, so much higher than cities or anxieties, and he whispered into my left ear, ''Of all my brothers and sisters, I'm the one your heartless century has wearied the most, ravaged the most. I am only Eros.''

My poor soul faltered, marvelling. He added, ''You saw me as a vulture, a jackal, I've been so hurt . . . Oh, I was only waiting to love you . . . Finally, you're here, finally, you're here for me . . .''

His voice sounded as if it had been drawn up from the depths of ages, but it was tender enough to make you weep. I kissed him at the base of his throat, then over all his face. I traced the corners of his lips and ran my hands through his hair dark with secrets. He laughed and his laughter opened out like a cluster of comets, and I laughed too because I'd lost my whole burden of pain. His belly quivered against mine. Ivy and cypress at once, we each wrapped a leg around the other's waist. I opened up onto his lance of joy, and our bodies' cantata rose up in powerful tendrils, sky and sea and flesh entangled, all the echoes of the earth suddenly voiceless, the tortured losing their distress, the bombs losing their roars, and I discovered, I discovered that in the face of evil there is nothing but love, the love so close to me, within me, and later, infinitely later, he said, "I chose you especially for your words, the words you write in darkness and doubt . . . There are so few who celebrate me now. Let me love you, love you forever, even if it will always be in the most complete darkness . . ."

◆

Fate will not have the last word with me.

To make room, I threw out all my old shoes the next morning. Then, sitting on the floor in the corner that was now of considerable interest, I discussed the situation with Chansonette. We came to an agreement: nothing is irrevocable and the twentieth century still has something beautiful about it.

I ransacked all the boutiques on St-Laurent. I tried on almost a thousand pairs, and bought the darkest ones I could find.

For Eros, always, I will not be seen anymore without my sunglasses.

◆

Fairy Rose

Since the birds don't fly up as high as my balcony, I always leave the highrise I live in to feed them bread at noon. That's the only time the triangular square next door gets the sun, if there is any. My pigeons are just as edgy as the crowd fighting its way through the traffic. I can identify each one of them much more easily than I can people. With time, I've managed to convince myself that they recognize me too, and that they like me. You get your affection wherever you can.

That's when she came to sit down next to me on the public bench. I thought, ''What a nerve,'' for normally nobody dares come near me when I'm feeding them. Well, because she was old and November was chilling us, I didn't protest. My friends, who had flown away in a flutter of reproach, returned. Albert was the first to fly back — he's the leader of the group — and then Anselme, who's been around, but hasn't lost his appetite.

The old girl didn't smell too good and she had a rusty metal cart in tow, full of all kinds of odds and ends. I pretended not to see her, for I don't want to be responsible for anyone at all, but she touched my arm to ask me for a cigarette. That brought us closer: I like women who smoke, they have the same taste for death that I do.

"Tell me, if you had one wish, what would it be?"

What an odd voice, too light, too playful, and enunciating too meticulously. It was a voice from a much earlier century, when there was still gentleness in life for some. The woman's voice was in absolute contrast to her twisted, crevassed, greyish face. I didn't answer for a moment because it's been a long time since I've had anything to wish for. To avoid the question, I said, "Why do you ask?"

"Because I'm a fairy, of course."

Yannick, the youngest, clucked knowingly and I saw he was far from convinced. So, not to be outdone, I wryly said, "A fairy? Fairies must be pretty poor these days."

She drew on her cigarette with great pleasure, nothing seemed to bother her, or hurry her.

"My dear, fairies decide on how they want to look. Honestly, what would I look like in my moon-coloured tulle dress in these grey surroundings? Besides that would be reason enough to have me locked up, wouldn't it? So, please, have you got a wish?"

That was a pretty good argument and even Thomas came closer to listen. But I need more than that. If I believed in fairies, I'd believe in God, and I'm not the believing type, I'm the despairing type. So I lit up another cigarette, I've got a blast-lighter, and hissed, "Prove it!"

She gave a strange throaty laugh and gestured with her hand. In an instant, the statue of Norman Bethune, all the pigeons, the bench, the old woman, and I all found ourselves in the heart of an orangery, in an air so soft I almost cried, and a sky clear enough and blue enough to kill. I was suffocating in my heavy clothes and the scent of sugar and damp earth filled the air. In the distance there was chanting accompanied by the crystalline sounds of a flute. I quickly picked the orange hanging nearest to see if all this was actually real. It was a blood orange, the kind I find most touching because of their colour of raw flesh. I bit into it and recalled a spring day when I was little. I had skipped school and freedom still tasted real. I closed my eyes. This was no fairy. She must be a sorceress to have awakened those memories in me.

The cold and the noise brought me back to reality. We were all back in this country that's in mourning for itself. My friends, especially Albert, observed me with round eyes. I really was on the spot now. I had to respond to the old woman's offer. I hadn't a minute to lose with her.

At first I thought I should wish for love-forever: you accumulate a number of sorrows and it's an immediate reflex, especially when you meet a real fairy. I began dreaming of a man who would love me and whom I would love; after all it would be acceptable, even pleasant to wake up in the morning and smile at someone happy to wake up with me, to fall asleep caressing his cashmere skin, to let myself reveal the blackest part of my soul to him, to joke with him, and make love with him, his gaze resting on mine, as he takes my head in his hands, and my body is wrapped around his. I thought about all that and was nostalgic for the kind of vulnerability you feel when you're no longer ashamed of your scars and you forgive yourself all your pain since joy has become possible.

I was thinking about all that and then I had second thoughts, and I told myself off for being selfish. If I had only one wish, then I'd have to wish for the destruction of everything nuclear, so I could stop having nightmares, humanity could have a future, and children would no longer be afraid to be born or to grow up.

But getting rid of nuclear power wouldn't reduce the disparity between North and South. Ethiopia would continue to die of starvation and Afghanistan to fight on against its Soviet invaders, while Poland suffocated under the same boot. South America would suffer its dictator-ships and South Africa lie dying in its apartheid horror, not to mention all the other peoples who are throttled that I've forgotten. I got quite dizzy thinking about such great collective distress. What should I choose? What would be the best wish for the whole world?

It all started surging through my head: make the handicapped mobile again, give the sick their health, wipe out loneliness, poverty, unhappiness, eliminate the custom of excision, get rid of lies forever. I grew sick at heart that I had only one little wish and so many responsibilities.

It was Anselme who got impatient and pecked my hand to remind me that the fairy might not wait around forever.

She'd finished her cigarette, so I lit another one for her with my lighter, and it was very odd, the flame seemed more iridescent than usual.

That's how it happened, looking at the old woman in her undefinable clothes, that I got the idea of the century, the solution of the century. I drew a deep breath, and slowly said, "Here's my wish — turn me into a fairy."

What had I said? She turned livid, began trembling, suddenly her magic aura dissipated and she was nothing but a disgusting baglady with rotten teeth, stinking of booze. She seized my hand, and mumbled, "Wait a minute, wait. You have no idea — being a fairy is no bed of roses. Before I grant your wish let me show you what it means, through *my* eyes."

Some kind of electric current passed right through me and everything I could see, everything around me, completely lost colour, became monochrome grey on grey, and then began swirling about. I saw my pigeons die and be replaced by others that hardly took notice of me before they themselves died. I saw buildings burn and collapse, and others rise in their places. I saw the crowd grow old and also die, yet continue running about pointlessly. It was a nightmare, a real life-sized nightmare. I yelled, "Help!" Everything returned to normal and the old lady's tired eyes were full of tears.

"There you go, a fairy can never die. Do you really want to be transformed?"

At that moment I understood that death is a mercy, that time only has its savour at that price, and that my unhappiness is quite impermanent because I am alive.

I took the fairy into my arms to console her. Finally I answered her, "Go and give your wish to someone else. Someone who needs it more than I do, OK?"

And so she left, with my birds, now calm again, around her head like a halo.

But ever since, every time I use my lighter, I hear a complicitous, throaty laugh.

Montreal, 1983–1988